FALLEN CREST CHRISTMAS

TIJAN

DEDICATION

This was written as a gift to any Fallen Crest readers out there! I hope you enjoy!!!

1

imeline is right after Fallen Crest University and before where Logan's book will pick up.

"HEY."

Sam looked up from the couch where she was sitting, in the basement, or more appropriately *still* in the basement. Mark came out of his bedroom and stopped in surprise at seeing her. His hand was raised, going through his hair, but he let it fall back to his side. He asked, "Can't face the music?"

A burst of voices sounded from the floor above them and they both looked up. Mark was referring to the Christmas gathering that his mother, her stepmother, had planned.

She let out a short laugh. "Yeah. How'd you figure?" A wry grin tugged at the corners of her lips as she raised her hand, holding a glass of Bourbon in it.

"Mason and Logan aren't here yet?" He came around the end and sank down on the other side of the couch. It was a long curved couch, so Sam was still positioned in the opposite side of the room as she stared back at him.

She shook her head. "They went to Helen's this morning. When she found out that not only was Garrett coming tonight, but Analise and James too, she changed her mind. Said she wanted to do her own thing, with her own kids, and I believe she's heading to Paris tonight."

Mark chuckled, leaning back against the cushion. "Never thought I'd say this about Mason and Logan's prissy mom, but that was smart of her."

Sam grunted, finishing the rest of her drink. She looked at it and sighed. Now she'd have to get up and walk towards the bar. That would entail moving. That would entail she'd have to get her ass up from the couch. Going to get a drink wasn't the problem. She was scared that once she stood up, Malinda would magically know and would open the basement door. She'd call down to them to come up and be 'social' and because Sam loved her stepmother, she would go upstairs. The problem--she couldn't 'face the party' as Mark had said. There were people up there that Sam didn't want to see, or she just wasn't ready to. She was taking a page from Logan's book and she was waiting till she had a good buzz before heading up there. Because she had that irrational thought of Malinda sensing when she stood up, she was good with staying in place. Her ass remained sitting.

Mark had been watching her and he laughed now. "Come on." He stood up and held his hand out. "I'll fill you up again."

She tensed up, but relaxed at his last statement. "Oh my God. I'll love you forever, Mark."

Taking the glass, Mark laughed again and shook his head, going to the bar in the corner of the room. "No, thank you. I don't want that. I am good with our brotherly/sisterly bond." Reaching for a second glass, he glanced up and caught her eyes. A look passed between them and Sam found herself smiling for real. It wasn't forced or in panic. She liked Mark. With all the craziness she'd endured over the last few years, having a nice stepbrother had been an unexpected icing on the cake, but she knew what he meant. Nope. There wasn't anything more than a friendship and step-sibling bond between them. If there were, she shuddered at the drama that would've been. She sighed, relaxing even more. "Yeah, Mason would not be happy with that."

Mark filled her glass, and brought it over, along with holding one for himself too. After handing it to her, he sank back onto his seat. "Oh yeah. Between Mason and Logan, I'd probably end up in the hospital at some point."

"They're not that bad." She sipped her drink, then thought about what she just said. "Nevermind. You totally would."

Mark laughed, taking a big drink from his glass. "I have no wish of landing on their shit list, never did."

She'd been lifting her glass back to her mouth, but paused and lowered it. "Is that why you were always kinda friendly with Logan? Even back during our sophomore year when I was still at Fallen Crest Academy?"

The corners of his mouth turned in, like he was holding back a laugh. He shrugged, looking sheepish. "Yeah. Kinda. I always got along with Logan, but once it came out how close you were with them, and I knew the hard-on that Adam had for you, let's just say I had to be careful at times. Going against the Kades is a dumbass move and Adam knew that, but Adam is Adam. I love the guy, but it was obvious you were going to end up with Mason. Fuck. Everyone knew that. People just had a hard time accepting it, for whatever reason."

Mark's mother hadn't began dating Sam's father until the next year. At the time, neither hadn't realized how they would be tied together, but Sam was grateful. When she started dating Mason and became 'family' with Logan too, things had been tense before she transferred from Fallen Crest Academy to Fallen Crest Public School, where Mason and Logan both attended. There'd been verbal confrontations, more than a handful of showdowns, and a couple punches thrown. Thinking about it now, she asked, "They never did anything bad, did they? Like setting anyone's car on fire or anything like that?"

Mark tossed back the rest of his drink, and grimaced. "That burned." He focused on her again. "Nah. They never did stuff like that. That was only against the Roussou peeps." He shook his head. "Budd Broudou never knew what he was signing up for, going against Mason and Logan."

Sam had to agree. The four year rivalry between the schools, Fallen Crest Public School and Roussou had been dangerous. Thinking back on it, she was surprised nothing horrible happened to either of them. She shuddered at that thought, but thinking back over the last few years with their recent battle against Park Sebastian, she knew she should be thankful nothing happened to any of them, herself included.

"Mark?" The door leading to the basement opened and Malinda called down, "Samantha?"

They shared another look. It was time to face the music.

Sam finished the rest of her drink and Mark lifted his up, but it was already empty. He groaned. "How about shots?"

He stood up and she held her empty glass to him. "Sounds good to me."

Taking both, he crossed to the bar and called upstairs, "We'll be up in a few, mom."

The door closed, but instead of returning to the gathering, Malinda came downstairs. Sam followed Mark. He went around the bar and she was standing between two of the barstools. Both turned around when Malinda came to the bottom of the stairs. She stopped, fixed them both with narrowed eyes, and rested her hand to her hip.

They waited, unsure how she'd proceed.

She laughed and snorted at the same time. "Well, fix me one too, my adorable son."

Sam had been holding her breath. She let it out now, giving

Malinda a shaky grin as her stepmother came to stand next to her. Malinda put an arm around her shoulders and squeezed her to her side. "Oh honey." She brushed a strand of Sam's hair back, tucking it behind her ear. "I am so sorry about your mother."

And the real reason why Sam couldn't bring herself to walk up those stairs was just named. Analise Stratton, who still shared Sam's last name even though it would be changing to Kade once she married Mason and Logan's father, James Kade, had invited herself to the family Christmas gathering upstairs. In fact, after arriving on Malinda and Sam's father's doorstep a week ago, Analise had declared she was 'back' in a lot of other ways. She spent a long stint at a group home, but was released because she was believed to be 'ready' and 'capable' of returning to her normal life outside of the group home setting.

And that meant she was ready to be Sam's mother again, or she was going to try. That was how she put it the night she arrived. Since then, Sam had nothing to do with her. Analise called every day. Sam ignored the calls every day. She came over twice more afterwards until Malinda had a private word with Analise. Sam hadn't been able to overhear the entire conversation. She'd come in the back door from a long run and stopped short before going out in the kitchen. Once she heard her mother's voice, she froze, but then heard Malinda saying, "...you have to let her come to you."

"But she never will." Analise sounded impatient. "I just want my girl back."

"You've been gone for almost two years, and before that you hurt her." Malinda remained strong, but comforting at the same time. "You can't come back in and make her want a relationship with you again."

"Because she's been brainwashed. That's why--"

Sam immediately tensed, hearing the anger in her mom's voice, but Malinda spoke up, "Now, you stop." Her voice dipped low, as if she moved closer to Analise. "No one has brainwashed that child against you, but she's an adult herself. She's in college, Analise, and whether you like it or not, Samantha will make up her own mind if she wants a relationship with your or not. It took me an entire year for her to warm up to me and I've been here. She lived with me her senior year of high school."

"And thank you for that."

Sam blinked, startled at the sudden switch in her mother's voice. She sounded genuinely grateful.

"Look," Malinda added. "Just give her time. Give her space. Let her come to you."

"I want to see her for Christmas."

A knot formed in Sam's stomach. She shifted, turning towards the opened doorway and pressed a hand to the wall. She went back to holding her breath.

There was a moment of silence before Malinda cleared her throat. "Well..."

"She's my daughter, Malinda." Analise sounded firm.

"I get that, but maybe I could have a small gathering. Everyone in the family could come here instead. Sam might feel more safe that way, and not so forced into a small intimate thing."

"You think she would?"

"I think..." Malinda seemed to be choosing her words with caution. "I think... you'll have a better chance at having some form of conversation with her if it happened here."

"I don't want Mason or Logan here--"

Malinda carried on as if she didn't hear that part, "--and especially if Mason and Logan are here too."

Sam bit down on her lip. The knot loosened up, but she wasn't becoming less tense. It was loosening up with anger. Her blood was heating up. Her mother dared come in here, dared to demand a holiday with her, and dared to demand Mason and Logan not be there? The two people who had been there for her over the last few years? Her fingers dug into the wall, but she was blind to how her nails would leave marks.

"Those boys hate me."

"Well, they have reason." Malinda let out a breath. "You hurt someone they both love. They protect her fiercely."

"And they've brainwashed her against me--"

"Analise, you have to stop. You can't think of them that way."

"How should I--no. You're right. My therapists said the same thing. They're her family. They took care of her when I couldn't. I have to remember that." A brief, but broken-sounding laugh came from Sam's mother. "They've had her when I haven't. I only focus on that sometimes, but you're right. I need to thank them for loving her and protecting her."

"Mmm hmm. I think that's the best way of handling both of those boys, and they aren't boys anymore either. They're men. And they're going to be in her life forever."

"I know. I do. I'm sorry. I've tried reaching out to Mason, but he won't return my calls."

Malinda barked out a genuine laugh. "Oh honey. I'm sorry, but you have a better chance at talking to your daughter than that one. If you want some advice, I'd apologize to both of those boys. Thank them for loving Sam, and leave it at that. I wouldn't hold my breath for any forgiveness or acceptance from either of them. Hell, I wouldn't hope for anything other than civil silence from them. That's all you're going to get."

"Yeah..." Her mother grew silent. "I suppose."

"Listen," Malinda said louder, and with a forced cheerfulness. "I'll talk to Sam, make sure the small gathering is okay with her, but I really think that's your only shot of spending the holidays with your daughter."

"And after that?"

"And...after that, give her time. You can't force a relationship. You have to let it unfold, but both parties need to want the relationship. She has to want it, too."

"I know. Okay." Analise drew in a breath, letting out a shaky laugh. "Thank you, Malinda. You've been so wonderful about this whole thing. Thank you for all the visits too."

"Of course. Okay. Sam went on a run and if I know her, she'll be coming home soon. I'd not be here if I were you."

"Okay. Call me about the party, though."

"I will."

A moment later, the door opened and then closed. Sam suddenly felt exhausted all over again. She didn't think it had anything to do with her hour-long run either. She held still, still standing just inside the doorway and waited until Malinda came back into the kitchen. As she did, her stepmother looked at her. Sam saw the prepared guardedness on Malinda's face. She knew Sam had been there the whole time.

Sam sighed, dropping her hand from the wall. "You've been to see her?"

Malinda reached up and rubbed at her forehead. The lines were tense around her eyes and her mouth was strained. "I have. It was a condition from her therapists. I'm sorry we never told you, honey."

Sam frowned. She wasn't sure how she felt about that, but she jerked up a shoulder. "I guess it makes sense. Better for you to deal with than me."

"I know." Malinda's hand went from her own forehead to Samantha's. She rubbed her thumb over it. "Oh, Samantha. You shouldn't have any of these worry lines."

Sam didn't pull away and when Malinda pulled her in tight for a hug, she went, but she didn't raise her arms to hug her back. The numbness that had always been there when she dealt with her mother was creeping in once more. It was low. It lined the bottom of her stomach, but Sam knew it would never go away, not while Analise was back. It had thawed over time, when Analise went away, but it was back.

Malinda hugged her and whispered, "Your mother will never hurt you. I won't let her. David won't either." She pressed a kiss to

Sam's forehead before stepping back. Her hand was still on Sam's shoulder. "But I have to ask about the holiday thing. Are you okay with that? I figured it was the best way to make sure you feel safe and she won't raise a ruckus, trying to force you to do something you don't want. We both know that'd end in a huge fight, one that she'd lose, but it would just be a pain in the ass for you to deal with."

Malinda was right. Sam realized it then, that Malinda was trying to prevent a line to be drawn. And Analise would've done exactly that. She would've tried to force Sam to see her. Sam wouldn't have done what her mother wanted and it would be a battle all over again. Sam nodded, trying to force a smile back to her stepmother. She murmured, "Thank you. Yes, I'm okay with it."

Malinda smiled back, though it still seemed tense. "Just keep Mason and Logan at your side. You'll be protected. Your mother's scared of those two."

And that was the plan, except both of them were still at Helen's. Sam gazed at Malinda now, as Mark pushed a shot into her hands. Analise arrived an hour ago, but no Mason and no Logan were present. Sam knew that was why no one ventured down to the basement to ask her to come up, but she knew the clock was ticking, hence why she'd been waiting for Malinda to sense she was walking around the basement. She'd have to go up there at some point in the evening.

She watched as Mark and his mother both had a shot. She already took hers, and now she was starting to feel the alcohol. This was ridiculous. She was in college. Her mother hadn't been able to hurt her for years...she shouldn't be scared of her, not after all the shit she had faced being in Mason and Logan's lives. But she had a feeling that no matter her age, no matter where she was in her life, there'd always be a little girl inside of her whenever she would see Analise.

She took a breath and rolled her shoulders back.

Enough was enough. She needed to shove that little girl inside to a corner because Analise couldn't have this much control over her. Not anymore.

She said, "I'm ready."

Malinda watched her gravely. "Are you sure?"

Mark put down the Bourbon bottle. "Even though Mason and Logan aren't here?"

She nodded, though her neck muscles had tightened up. "I'm sure." The booze was warming her up too. "Helps that I got a little buzz going too."

Mark grinned. "Well, okay." He came around the bar and nodded towards the stairs. "Until Mason and Logan show up, I'll be at your side."

"Me too."

They both arched their eyebrows up at Malinda. She gave them a sheepish grin. "Well, until my hostessing duties pull me away."

Mark chuckled, putting his arm around his mom's shoulder. "No worries, Mom. I know that I've just gotta get you liquored up enough and you'll be giving Analise an earful all on your own."

"Well, I have been nice to her, a lot nicer than I wanted to be." She looked and held Sam's gaze. "But you let me know if it's too much. Your mother is allowed in this house only because I understand her pain, from mother to mother, but if she hurts you at all, I'll kick her out. I've held my tongue more than I usually do with her."

"I will." Sam nodded. "Okay. Let's go. Let's get it over with."

The three of them went upstairs.

As they left the peace and quiet from the basement, they stepped into a Christmas wonderland. Malinda had decorated the house over the weekend, but with the lights turned down and the Christmas lights lighting the room, Sam was struck by how beautiful the entire first floor was. It wasn't just the living room, but also the kitchen and dining room. All of the counters in the kitchen and the table in the dining room were covered in food. There were platters of meat, cheese, crackers, vegetables, and fruit. A few warmers were placed in the center of the table with lids over top. At one end of a counter was where the drinks were placed. A large bowl was set up, along with canisters for hot cider, cocoa, and tea.

"You got a bartender, Mom?" Mark craned his neck, seeing into the screened in porch that was attached on the other end of the kitchen.

"Yes, but I think you've had enough, my darling son that I still want to be a darling tonight."

Mark chuckled, saying under his breath, "I think I'm the last of your worries tonight, Mom."

Hearing the sudden alertness in his voice, Sam stiffened, and glanced up. His gaze was fixed past the kitchen and to the entryway. And there, just coming in the front door, wasn't the reason why she'd been tense, but the reason why she experienced a rush of warmth.

Mason and Logan both walked in, and both met her gaze, gave her a smile, but trailed past her shoulder. Their easygoing grins instantly strained and their eyes grew cold.

Sam knew, she felt their coldness adding to the numb lining of her stomach, even before she heard those two words spoken behind her.

"Hi, Samantha."

2

She couldn't look away from Mason.

His hair was wet, like he just showered, and he had already taken off his coat so his shoulders looked even wider, but so delicious under his navy shirt. Logan stood next to him, both looking crisp and on high alert. As Mason continued to hold her gaze, she saw from the corner of her eye as Logan moved towards them. She told them both her mother was coming, but it'd been a week since either of them saw Analise, and that night hadn't ended well. She readied herself for whatever was going to come next. As she did, Logan stopped right in front of her. Mason came behind him. She was still staring up at her boyfriend's gaze. If she could, she would've taken his strength in her because she was already sapped of it.

Only Analise. Only her mother could do this to her.

Then, she heard Logan drawl, "Well, hell. The psycho bitch from the psycho ward has officially entered the building." He glanced to Malinda and flashed a smirk. There was a hard edge to it. "What's up with this, Mama Malinda? I didn't think you were down with peeps who like to hurt Samantha."

Analise drew in a breath as Malinda said, "Come on, Logan.

You were told she was coming. I'd expect some decency from you."

"Nope." Logan shook his head, his smirk growing. "I see the Anabitch and my jackass side comes out."

"Logan."

He glanced back to Mason, who had spoken. Logan asked, "Don't tell me you're okay with this."

Mason shook his head. "I'm not, but it's not our call."

He cast Sam a meaningful look and Logan let out a small growl. "Are you fucking kidding me? Analise scares the shit out of Sam. It's our job to be the jerkoffs. We're doing it for her."

"We're also not in high school anymore."

Logan let out a disgruntled sound, but made a point of swinging his head to Sam. "It's your call, I guess. You want me to tear her apart or should I leash the asshole?"

Before Sam could respond, Malinda moved forward. She stepped between Sam and Logan, placing a hand on his shoulder and turned him around. She spoke, "You're going to leash the asshole and you're going to go somewhere else because this is my home. If, and that's only if, Sam needs someone to step up for her, I'll get the pleasure of kicking someone out of my home." She emphasized the 'my' before walking away with Logan. Before they were out of earshot, Sam heard Malinda say, "You just got here and I already feel like another drink."

Logan chuckled. "It's my charm, Mama Malinda."

"God help us then."

Mason moved forward so he was standing in front of Sam, but while he reached out and linked their hands, neither said a word. He looked over to Mark and raised an eyebrow.

"Oh." Mark's eyes widened. He coughed and laughed. "Uh, yeah. I think..." He jerked around, pointing around the room. "Oh yeah. I'm needed over there, next to the...uh, yeah. I'm going for a drink too."

As he hurried away, Mason and Sam turned as one. They were standing side by side as both faced against Analise.

Samantha stared at her mom for a moment. She looked different this night compared to the other times Analise stopped by the house. There'd been a desperation clinging to her mother, but this mother, she looked composed. Calm. Almost serene, in a small way. Sam frowned, not seeing the beautiful white dress her mother was dressed in, how it was so similar to the black dress Sam wore, or how her mother's long black hair was pulled up in a braid, much the same as her own hair. She wasn't seeing that she was almost a spitting image of Analise. All she was seeing was the memories over the years and the reminder of how her mother threatened to ruin Mason's life.

Sam could only see that last night, when she told her mom to go to hell. The feeling of walking away, having an empty pit in her stomach and feeling the hole inside of her, the one that only a mother should've filled, widened instead of closed. But when she fixed a polite smile on her face and murmured, "Hello," her mother had no clue of the agony Sam was feeling.

Mason did.

He glanced down at their hands. Sam's knuckles were white. She was clinging to him.

She said further, her tone almost light and casual, "Is James with you?"

Analise was studying her daughter, taking her all in. A look of wonder entered her eyes and she blinked, as if realizing her daughter asked a question. "Oh! Oh yes." She gestured to the living room. "He's over there." Her lips pressed against each other before she added, "I believe he's talking to Garrett." She said to Mason, "I didn't realize you guys were so friendly with Samantha's biological father."

Mason narrowed his eyes, but looked as well. Just like she said, his father was talking to both of Sam's fathers, her biological one and the one who raised her. He swung his gaze back to

Analise and fixed her with a polite fuck-you smile. "Looks like. David too. They all seem to be getting along, don't they?"

Analise's eyes mirrored his, narrowing. "It looks like."

Sam cleared her throat. "What do you want, Analise? Why are you here?"

"Samantha—" Analise started to laugh, even raising a hand to her throat.

Sam cut her off, scowling. "Cut the bullshit. You want a relationship with me? Is that it?"

The hand went back down. The fake smile dimmed and Analise's head moved back half an inch. She was reassessing her daughter. "I thought you were terrified of me."

"I am, but I've learned how to be a bitch while I want to crap my pants at the same time." Sam let go of Mason's hand and stepped forward. She leaned her head, angling so she was in her mother's face, standing on the exact same level. "You know I want nothing to do with you. Why are you here? Why are you forcing your presence on an entire house that wants nothing to do with you?"

Analise sucked in her breath, but replied a second later, "Because I am going to marry Mason and Logan's father. Because whether you or they believe me or not, I do love him and now that I am better, we are all going to be one big happy fucking family. That's why."

"So it's because of James?"

"It's because of everyone involved." Analise's shoulders dropped. Some of the tension left her. "Because I really do want to have a relationship with you and I want a civil relationship with them." She said to Mason, "I'm not going anywhere. I'd like peace between you and your brother and myself. I'd like to do that for your father."

"Then why didn't you want them here?" Sam asked.

Mason frowned.

Analise closed her eyes for a beat. She opened them again as her shoulders lifted up, taking in air. "Because it's easier to talk to you when they're not around. Because I know they'll always hate me so I was hoping to get a shot, just a small shot, of having a decent conversation with you." Her voice softened. "I wanted to apologize for all the hurt I caused you and I wanted to see if there's any chance, even the slightest, that you would be willing to start over again?"

A sheen of tears formed over Analise's eyes, but she didn't blink or look away. She held her daughter's gaze and waited for the answer.

Sam didn't say anything. Not for a second, then another, and another. More than ten seconds passed before her eyes dropped. She said, "No." She added, "Please leave." And then she walked away, her hand lifting to her own eyes as she brushed a tear away.

Mason remained behind, watching his girlfriend disappear back down to the basement. This would have ramifications. Even if Analise became a nun, he knew the type she was. Batshit crazy. That never went away. Analise was trying. He saw that. He recognized that, but he saw what she wasn't seeing. It wasn't going to work. The harder she pushed, the more Sam would go away.

She turned away, her jaw trembling, and she folded her arms over her chest.

He saw the damage Sam's words caused her too, and even though this woman wanted to ruin his life before and tried to take his girlfriend away, he knew tearing into her wasn't going to help anyone.

"You must be having a hay day," Analise clipped out. A tear broke free, sliding down her cheek. She ignored it. Her eyes flashed back at him, searing in anger.

He didn't say anything. He waited.

She added, "You and your brother have hated me since day one. You never gave me a shot." Her hand jerked out, indicated where Sam had gone. "And she wants nothing to do with me now. It's been like this all week."

"It's been like this all year," Mason corrected her.

She stiffened. Her gaze met his again.

He said further, "And the year before that." His head bowed a little bit, but his voice hardened. "And the year before that. And the year before that, but for those years, you didn't want to see the damage you were causing her. That's the only difference."

"I am going to marry your father."

He nodded. "I know. I've accepted that, so has Logan."

She let out a harsh laugh. "Really? You could've fooled me."

"You're misunderstanding some things here." He spoke softly, eerily softly. "If you want peace with all of us, for my father's sake, we can give that to you. We don't have to war against you, but that's not what you're coming in here for and that's not what you're pushing for. You're pushing for a relationship. There's a vast difference between peace and having a relationship. You cannot ask for a relationship. Not with your daughter. Not with your fiancé's sons. You cannot force something we will not give."

"So what am I supposed to do?"

"Nothing."

A bitter sound ripped from her throat. It was supposed to sound like a laugh, but it failed even that. She shook her head as a second tear fell. "I want my daughter back—"

"Then earn her back," Mason shot back. Logan was returning, weaving through the small crowd from the bar. His gaze was centered on them and he narrowed his eyes, raising a beer that he was bringing back for his brother. Mason held his hand out, but Analise didn't see it. She was half turned away, as if she would've gone after where Sam went. Her back was to where Logan was coming from and when he paused, lifting an eyebrow in question, Mason shook his head from side to side. He held up a finger, asking for a minute. Logan nodded, letting his hands lower back so they were in front of him. Mason added, speaking quietly but firmly, "Show her why she should want her mother back. Sam wants the same thing that she's always wanted since I've known her. She wants her family back, and yes, that's you too. She has Malinda, but Malinda's not you. She didn't raise Sam all her life."

Analise sucked in her breath. She blinked, letting more tears fall. "You think so?"

"She wants some type of relationship with you, yes, but if you try to force it, it'll never happen. Don't force it."

"So what? Do nothing?"

"Yes." The answer was so simple and Mason delivered it as soon as she asked that question. "Be polite to her. Be nice to her, but that's all you can do. You need to back off from her."

"That could take years."

"So it'll take years. Who cares?" His words were clipped again. "If you force it, it'll never happen. Ever. If you don't, it may happen. It's your choice in the end, but hear me right now. I want to be really clear." He waited until Analise turned so she was looking right into his eyes. He said then, "I'm older. Logan's older. That means we're smarter than we were and if you ever hurt your daughter again, we will ruin you and you'll have no idea how we even did it. Remember that."

Then, his eyes cut back to Logan's and he nodded, moving his head in the direction of the basement. He moved forward, leading the way. Logan came up behind him, and right before they moved through the party and slipped downstairs, Logan flashed Analise a grin. He chided under his breath to her, "Still hoping to get to know us again?"

3

"All right, Sam." Logan cocked his head to the side, a teasing grin on his face, as he sauntered down the stairs. Sam was at the bar, pouring herself a drink, when he stepped down and moved forward, right behind Mason. Logan added, "Did you stuff my stocking with a big dildo? Tell the truth."

Sam watched him. She didn't blink. She didn't move. She did nothing, except hold an empty glass in front of her. Then, she grinned back. "Yes, Logan. I've been wanting to ram a stick up your ass. You caught me. It was on my wish list this Christmas." She fanned herself. "Santa finally came this year."

Logan chuckled. "Came, you said?"

"Oh my God." Sam rolled her eyes and finished pouring herself a drink. She set it down, then eyed both of them as they slid onto the barstools. "What do you guys want?"

"No, no." Logan held out his hand. "Just give me the rum."

She grabbed an unopened rum bottle and started to twist it open.

Logan reached over and grabbed it from her, giving her another grin. "I meant the whole bottle." He wiggled his eyebrows at her. "Unlike you, Miss Samantha, I'm planning on making up Santa's entire naughty list...just tonight." He twisted the cap off and saluted the bottle in the air. "Bottoms up, mi familia. Feliz navi-don't."

Sam glanced to Mason and he pointed to one of the beer bottles and Sam opened it before handing it over. He asked her, "You okay?"

She lifted a shoulder up, gripping her glass once again with both hands. "It's whatever. I was prepared for her tonight, and it's over with now. So..." She shrugged again. "Yeah. Whatever. She's back..."

Mason watched his girlfriend, just like he watched all those years ago. He saw the same tonight that he saw on her face the first time she was going to be his roommate. Hurt. That's all Analise had done to Sam. Even trying to remember, he couldn't recall a time when Analise had been there for her daughter, or supported her how a mother should've. It had put him in an almost rage back then, though Sam never realized truly how deep his fury went. He remembered the night he, Logan, and Nate forced wine down Analise's throat. He cringed now at the memory, but it was what it was. Analise was trying to take Sam away from them. She was trying to hurt her even more and they stopped her. They showed her what they could do. It was a power play. They had the power. She needed to realize it, and now, all these years later, he knew Analise wouldn't fight the same way.

She hadn't been prepared for them to stand up to her. She narced on them, told their dad what they did, but it was all of them against her word. If they did something like that again, Analise would fight back with a better strategy. He saw that in her tonight. She was smarter. She was more 'sane', but that made her more calculating and more dangerous.

Maybe she really did want to have peace in the family. He did believe she loved his father. And it would make sense that she'd want a relationship with her daughter. That's what mothers did, right? Even the inept ones. Analise seemed like she was born with the natural love a mother had, but she was also born with her mental illness. He could be the nice son. He could be the nice boyfriend. Glancing at Logan, Mason considered even being the nicer role mentor, taking the high road.

Fuck that.

He wasn't the nice guy.

No. Even though, he said he'd play nice with her above and Sam really did want a relationship with her mother, Mason had no plans of letting Analise hurt his girlfriend again. Nope. He would watch, and wait. If anything she did had harmful consequences towards Sam, he was going to ruin his future stepmother once and for all.

She wasn't allowed to hurt her daughter. Not if he could help it.

"What are you planning?" Logan pointed at him with the rum bottle. His eyes narrowed and he started to shake his head from side to side. "I know that look. It's your calculating look." The corner of his mouth curved up. "I've missed that look."

Mason grinned back. "You saw it three weeks ago."

Logan shrugged, placing the rum onto the bar. "All this holiday cheer and 'be merry' attitude is making me feel constipated. It's making me want to shit on everything, literally. I figure we should do whatever you're planning instead. It'll be less messy."

Mason grew aware of Sam's focus. He met her gaze and saw the wariness in it. "I won't hurt her, not unless she hurts you first."

Her shoulders rose and her chest moved up as she took in a pocket of air. She didn't say anything, not at first. Then, her voice cracked and she murmured, "I told her I didn't want anything to do with her."

"But we all know that's bullshit."

She glanced to Logan. He added, "Come on, Sam. This is your mother. Our mom's hardly ever around again, but I can't deny

that there's a little boy inside of me who still wants her attention."
His tone quieted. "You can't deny that either, even to yourself."

"I'm not..." But she stopped.

She was.

Her head went down and her hands wrapped around the glass, holding it in a tight grip. The longer she took to respond, the tighter her grip grew. She jerked her head back up, a haunted expression hung over her. "I've never been more scared to let someone back in my life."

"So don't."

Logan and Sam both quieted, turning to Mason as he said those two simple words. He pressed against the bar, but he didn't reach for Sam's hands. He knew she would've recoiled, just because she didn't want to soften in that moment. She needed to remain hard. He said, "Don't let her in. If you decide at some point to try, then it'll be then. It doesn't have to be now. It doesn't have to be on her timeline. It's your call. Your decision. Your time. You control every aspect of it."

Logan snorted. "Analise is going to love that."

"I don't care," Mason threw at him. He narrowed his eyes. "If she starts piping up, we'll shut her up. We did it before. We can do it again."

Logan held his gaze, then swung to Sam. All three were silent for a moment, and in that shared quiet, it was three of them versus Analise. But it was more. It went deeper. It was them versus anyone who tried to hurt one of them. It was like this before. It was like this now, and it would be forever.

The door leading to the basement opened and Christmas music from above filtered down to their room. Mark's voice said, "They're down here...I think..." He came down and nodded. "Yep. At the bar. I guessed right."

Heather Jax followed him. A slow grin tugged the corner of her mouth up and she lifted up her hands. "I bring you good tidings and joy."

"Finally." Logan met her half way and took some of the bags. He carried them back to the bar. "What'd you bring us, Jax, and sidenote," he paused before opening a bag and winked at her, "How are you and Channing?"

She fixed him with a warning stare. "We're on again."

Logan wrinkled his nose. "So that means there's no chance of a 'you and me' being 'on' tonight either?"

"Not a chance."

"Just so you know, having a boyfriend is overrated."

"Why?" She leaned back and folded her arms over her chest. "Because I can't hook up with guys?"

"Because you can't hook up with *me*." He ran a hand down his chest, smirking. "I'm the Jack Sparrow of Christmas tonight. I've got Rum, my own sword, and the right attitude about your problem."

Heather closed her eyes, bit down on her lip, then let out a sigh. "I don't even want to ask, but I can't help myself." She looked at Logan. "What is my problem?"

"The question that will plaque you all your life." He leaned close and whispered, "Should I or should I not find out where Logan hung his stocking?"

Sam burst out laughing. Mason shook his head and Heather rolled her eyes. She held up a hand, placed it over Logan's face, and pushed him backwards. "I already know where your stocking is hung. Thank you, but the only thing I really want from you—" Her hand snaked down his arm and she grabbed the bottle from him. Brandishing it between them, she grinned. "—is the rum. Merry Christmas, Logan, but I'll never go down your chimney again."

Without missing a beat, Logan said, "Ho, ho, ho."

"Okay." Sam pressed her lips together, then cleared her throat. Going around the bar, she held her hands up and said, "Give me a hug. Holy shit, woman. I've missed you."

As Sam and Heather hugged, Logan opened one of the bags. "Holy crap, woman."

Heather pulled back, saw the reason for his statement. "Yeah." She grabbed one of the other bags and reached inside to pull out a forty ounce bottle of beer. Holding it up, she showed it off as if it were a prize. "One of the benefits from running the grill now, not that I didn't have the hook-up before, but whatever." She laughed, setting it down and pulling out another forty ounce bottle. The rest of the bags were opened. All held the same size bottle. She gestured to all of them. "Merry Christmas, fuckers. I'm keeping it classy this year. Forties for everyone."

Logan groaned, holding his tightly. His eyebrows pinched forward and he shook his head, his eyes scanning her up and down. "You bring me a forty ouncer. You dress in your little jean miniskirts, and you share my same dirty sexual humor. Why the fuck did Channing meet you first?"

Heather laughed, pressing a kiss to his forehead. She murmured before stepping back, "You and me would never work, Logan. I'd only bring out the dirty side of you."

"That's quite fine with me right now." He gazed down right into her eyes. "Sure you can't take a 'holiday' from Channing, just for the night?"

"I'm ignoring that, but Merry Christmas to one my favorite flings ever."

The two saluted each other, tapping their bottle necks to the other, before they both tipped their heads back and drank. As they did, Sam moved around the group and pressed against Mason's side. She burrowed into him and he adjusted, turning so his back was to the flirting two with Mark silently watching. His mouth was twisted into an awkward grimace. Taking Sam's hand, he pulled her back around the group and into her bedroom. Shutting the door, he leaned against it and pulled her towards him, holding both of her hands again.

She closed her eyes and rested her forehead to his chest.

Mason cupped the side of her face, tilting her backwards to look up at him. As he did, he said, "She won't hurt you. I won't let her."

A tear welled up, but it didn't fall. It held there, pooling in the corner of her eye. "Some hurts can't be prevented. Having a mother like that is just one of them."

Mason let out a groan, letting his head fall down so his forehead rested against her. "If I can prevent it, I will. I can promise that much. At least."

"I know." She lifted their hands so they were pressed between both of them. "Merry Christmas, Mason."

He laughed, his chest moving slightly, as he traced the side of her face. His finger swept up to her lips and lingered at the corner of them. "Merry Christmas, Samantha."

She smiled up, as his own lips mirrored her same expression. Then, she raised herself up on tiptoes and pressed her lips to his. She breathed into him, "I love you."

Mason didn't say it back. His lips took over and he locked the door behind them. He showed her, instead.

BONUS SCENE

T IMELINE: *AFTER FALLEN FOURTH DOWN AND BEFORE FALLEN CREST UNIVERSITY*

MASON WAS IN FALLEN CREST. I was in Boston. This Christmas was going to suck. I didn't even want to contemplate it as I laid in bed that morning. Garrett had been great. The entire trip to Boston, being flown first-class, getting picked up by him and his driver, spending the last few days in his apartment that was downtown in Boston. All of it was glamorous, in some effed-up way, but I didn't want to be there. I wanted to be in bed. I wanted to have woken up with Mason beside me.

"Samantha?" Garrett's voice came through the door.

I cursed under my breath, but called out, "Good morning." I didn't want to talk to him yet, but I didn't want him worried that something was wrong. He'd be knocking every five minutes asking if I wanted something to eat, something to drink, if he should order a movie, etc.

"It's Christmas today."

"Yep." Fucking great. "Merry Christmas."

"Uh, can you come out here? There's a surprise for you."

A small laugh left me. "I saw the Christmas tree. Those thirty presents aren't really surprises."

"No, I mean," he leaned back, and his voice grew muffled. I sat up, frowning, but then I heard him say, "Okay. Love you too." Then he leaned back closer to the door, his voice growing clear again. He said, "I'm making breakfast for us, but I have it on good authority that you like coffee too. There's a latte here. I don't want it to go cold."

"Oh." I sighed. That was really sweet of him. "Okay. I'll be out in a little bit."

"I'll hurry with the first batch of pancakes then."

As he left, I got dressed, but it was just Garrett and me. If I'd been at Fallen Crest, I would've put on jeans and a better top. Mason and Logan would've been at the house all day. Heather might've stopped over. Hell. Because of Mark, I was sure some of the Academites would've come as well. At this rate, I wouldn't have even minded them. When I headed for the kitchen, all I could think about was who I was missing at home. Tears were at my eyes, threatening to spill, but I could hear Garrett's voice. He was back on the phone and he sounded so damn happy. I stopped, right before the kitchen and took a breath. I was in Boston because Mason and Logan wanted me there. I was there for my safety in case of any fall-out from the house burning, but damn. It hurt. A lot.

I wanted to be with them.

But I wasn't. I was here, with my biological dad.

Forcing a smile on my face, I stepped into the kitchen. Garrett was smiling at me, a look of expectation in his eyes. I frowned. "What?"

He gestured towards the door. "There's your latte."

As I turned, I gasped. He was right—my latte was there and it was being held by Mason.

He was there. He was in Boston. He was right in front of me.

His eyes widened as he saw my intent. He had just enough time to put the coffee on the table beside him before I launched myself at him.

Wrapping my arms around his neck, my legs wound around his waist, and I burrowed into his chest. He was with me. That all I cared about. "Mason," I whispered, but I couldn't even say his name without choking. I stopped trying and I just held him.

His arms wrapped around my back and he held me. He whispered into the crook of my neck and shoulder, "I have a day to be with family. I have to fly back for football tomorrow."

One day. I got him for one day. I whispered against his chest, "I love you. Thank you for this."

He cupped the back of my head in a tender motion and whispered back, his lips grazing over my skin, "I love you back."

"Okay." Garrett cleared his throat from behind us. "I think— well, look at that. I'm completely out of flour and I have a sudden desire to make bread. So," I kept my head buried into Mason's chest, but I could hear Garrett moving around and then the door opened. He said, "I'm going to head out for a while. Get that flour and maybe some wine, don't tell your dad on me."

Mason chuckled and the sound of it warmed me, sliding inside of me and making everything all right. He swept a hand down my back and pressed his lips to my forehead again. Then he whispered, "As much as I'd like to bury myself in you, I can't do that to Garrett."

I clasped tighter to him. I didn't even care. Mason was there. He was in my arms. He was holding me. My Christmas was complete. I tipped my head back, meeting his eyes and I whispered, a small tear appearing at my eye, "Thank you for coming."

His eyes roamed over my face, a tender look in them, and his grin softened. "You're family. Where else would I go?" I was about to say Logan's name, when Mason shook his head. He said before I could, "I love my brother, but he's not you. There was no choice in my mind. It's you. It's always you."

I knew it was Christmas. I knew I was in Boston to spend time with my real dad and to be safe, away from any fall-out from the fraternity if they chose to reach out to Fallen Crest, but I didn't care about any of that right then. I wanted twenty-four hours of just Mason. No Garrett. No talk about anyone else. Just him and me and thinking about that, I slid down to the floor. He released me, but caught me at the last moment so I didn't hit the floor too hard. I took his hand, entangling our fingers and I led him to my bedroom.

"Sam," Mason started.

I shook my head and started grabbing clothes, then throwing them on the bed.

He paused in the doorway, watching me, as he braced himself with both his hands on the doorframe. He frowned. "What are you doing here?"

Stuffing enough to cover me for a day in a bag, I grabbed my shoes and a few toiletries, then I ducked underneath Mason's arm and went back to the kitchen. He followed me and waited as I scribbled a note to Garrett.

GARRETT—HEADED to a hotel. I get him for 24 hours. I'm not sharing with you. See you tomorrow at this time! Sam P.S. Merry Christmas! I'm really sorry.

DROPPING the pen beside the note, I grabbed my keys, phone, coat, and then Mason's hand again. I pulled him out the door and we headed down for the street. As we stepped to the curb, I lifted my arm and signaled for a cab. Mason asked, "Are you sure about this?"

I nodded as a taxi slid to a stop beside us. When we got in, after I gave him the name of a hotel, I said to Mason, "Twenty-four hours. I want just you and me."

Mason nodded and I saw the relief on his face. I understood it, to an extent. Because Garrett was taking care of me, Mason felt some sort of respect to him, like he owed him and being with me under his roof wasn't the nicest way to thank a guy for watching his girlfriend. When we had talked about Boston, if I should go or not, Mason kept insisting. I understood from his point of view. Sebastian could go to Fallen Crest. They could hurt me, even there, but if I was in Boston, they might not reach out to me here. But I had been surprised that Mason was okay with me being here with Garrett and he explained one night, when we in bed, "The guy's a douche, but he didn't know about you. When he did, he came to see you."

"But he left me."

"He went back home to get his wife and make his family right again. Then he came again for his daughter." He shrugged, playing with my fingers and gazing at the ceiling. "A part of me respects that. He's trying to make his home solid for his kid. Dating my mom, that wasn't the right way to start a relationship with your daughter, you know?"

He turned to look at me then and I didn't see the slight respect he had for Garrett. I saw the father he would be. It took my breath away. I knew, I felt it then, that Mason would do anything for his child. No matter the circumstances, he would make his home life strong, just how he described, so his child would feel the security a child should only feel.

I started crying and he lifted a hand to my eye, wiping it away. "What's wrong?"

I shook my head. I couldn't talk for a moment. Mason would be the father the he hadn't had, that I hadn't gotten. My love for him swelled even more in me and I grinned, whispering, "I love you. That's all. No, that's not all. I love you even more."

He frowned. "Why?"

"Just because." Because of who you are. That's why. But I didn't say those words. I kept them to myself and I leaned close to touch my lips to his. He swept me over him and deepened the kiss. No words were shared after that, not for a long while as I showed him how much more I loved him.

He kissed me now, bringing me back to reality, and I looked up to see that we were at the hotel. It was a classy one. I knew Garrett had mentioned it a few times when he said if anyone came to visit, he would have them stay here so when we approached the front desk, I used Garrett's name. The hotel was so nice that I doubted we would've gotten a room otherwise and it worked. My dad's name got the front desk attendant's attention and we were given a room key moments later.

When we got into the room, I didn't have time to look around. Mason swept me up and carried me to the bed, or maybe I swept him up. Our lips met and we didn't talk for a long time, a very long time. Okay, we didn't talk for the rest of the night. We didn't sleep either. It was spent exploring each other's bodies, showing our love, remembering how it felt to be with one another. The first time when he slid inside of me, I closed my eyes and savored the moment. Home. Mason was home. He was family. He was the future.

He was my soulmate.

IT WAS SHORT, but I hope you all enjoyed!